Contents

1. A Magical Transmission   9

2. The Box in Mr. Pilma's Office   15

3. It's a Have-To   33

4. The Race of the StarCruiser Ultimate XR   39

5. A Problem Solved   47

6. The Calming Cape   55

7. The "Super Risa" Solution   63

8. The Word Launcher   71

9. Attack of the Laser Scissors   87

10. Making Mistakes is Part of Learning (The Hard Part)   97

11. Taking Off the Cape   109

Baj and the Word Launcher

of related interest

fiction

Anne Droyd and Century Lodge
Will Hadcroft
ISBN 1 84310 282 X

Blue Bottle Mystery
An Asperger Adventure
Kathy Hoopmann
ISBN 1 85302 978 5

Of Mice and Aliens
An Asperger Adventure
Kathy Hoopmann
ISBN 1 84310 007 X

Lisa and the Lacemaker
An Asperger Adventure
Kathy Hoopmann
ISBN 1 84310 071 1

Haze
Kathy Hoopmann
ISBN 1 84310 072 X

Buster and the Amazing Daisy
Nancy Ogaz
ISBN 1 84310 721 X

picture books

Different Like Me
My Book of Autism Heroes
Jennifer Elder
Illustrations by Marc Thomas and Jennifer Elder
ISBN 1 84310 815 1

Different Croaks for Different Folks
All About Children with Special Learning Needs
Midori Ochiai
With notes on developmental differences by Shinya Miyamoto
Illustrated by Hiroko Fujiwara
Translated by Esther Sanders
ISBN 1 84310 392 3

Baj and the Word Launcher

Space Age Asperger Adventures in Communication

Pamela Victor

Jessica Kingsley Publishers
London and Philadelphia

First published in 2006
by Jessica Kingsley Publishers
116 Pentonville Road
London N1 9JB, UK
and
400 Market Street, Suite 400
Philadelphia, PA 19106, USA

www.jkp.com

Library of Congress Cataloging in Publication Data
Victor, Pamela, 1966-
Baj and the word launcher : space age Asperger adventures in communication / Pamela Victor.
    p. cm.
ISBN-13: 978-1-84310-830-6 (pbk.)
ISBN-10: 1-84310-830-5 (pbk.)
    1. Autistic children—Language—Juvenile literature. 2. Asperger's
syndrome—Patients—Language—Juvenile literature. 3. Communicative
disorders in children—Juvenile literature. 4. Interpersonal communication—Juvenile literature.   I. Title.
RJ506.A9V53 2006
618.92'858832—dc22

                                        2006012370

British Library Cataloguing in Publication Data
A CIP catalogue record for this book is available from the British Library

ISBN-13: 978 1 84310 830 6
ISBN-10: 1 84310 830 5

Printed and bound in Great Britain by
Athenaeum Press, Gateshead, Tyne and Wear

This book is dedicated to
Jeff, Jake, and Sierra.

My love, my heart, my soul.

Chapter One

A Magical Transmission

The flying bicycle was slowly lowered to its parking space in the suspended garage outside Baj's house. Sitting astride the bike, Baj pressed the button on the flying bike to increase its gravitational field and an airy hiss signaled the complete docking of the bike.

Baj jumped off and tossed his helmet toward the hovering cabinet nearby. He missed, and his helmet floated alone around the garage. Later, Baj's mom would make him return to the garage to put his helmet away, but right now Baj was too excited to stop. He ran up toward his sleeping quarters with his backpack clutched to his chest.

"Hi, Baji!" his dad popped his head out of his office. "Your snack is on the kitchen table. I'm in the middle of a meeting with the managers on the Second Moon of Neri. Can't talk now."

"Thanks, Dad," Baj called back over his shoulder. "I'll be in my room for a while!"

"OK, buddy." Baj's dad flipped on his holo-gramphone as he popped back into his office. Baj knew that his dad had to concentrate when he was speaking Neridian. On Baj's home planet of Anlar, they spoke Aurlian, which to Baj seemed very similar to Neridian, but for some reason it was harder for his dad to speak interplanetary languages. As he zipped down the hallway, Baj thought about how some things were so much easier for him to learn than for other people. He felt lucky to have such a great memory.

Standing outside his room, Baj poked his finger into the Identifier which was fitted out-side the door of his sleeping quarters. With a soft whoosh, the door slid open. Baj quickly checked the Identifier screen. It read:

```
"Approved entry:
11:03am–11:16am…
User identified as VacuumBot.
Unapproved entry attempted:
2:18pm…User identified as
User 5. Risa. Entry denied.
End of transmission."
```

"Awesome!" Baj said, tossing his backpack onto his bed. He had readjusted the Identifier to reject his sister Risa's fingerprint. Now she could never sneak into his room and mess up his stuff while he was at his after school meeting with Mr. Pilma. "Great job, Identifier."

"Confirmation of message, Baj," the Identifier responded in a halting voice. "Continue entry denial of User 5?"

"A big yes on that one!" Baj answered the machine. Baj didn't really mind sharing his stuff with his sister, Risa. It's just that last week she had snuck into his room and played with his model of the solid rainbow over the planet

Eshrira, and she'd broken off a piece of the crystal quartz. Baj just wanted to teach her a lesson about asking him before she borrowed something from his room.

Beep da beep da beep.

The hologramphone rang in Baj's room.

"Who's calling?" Baj asked.

"User 12: Anda," replied the h-phone. Anda had been Baj's best friend since they were three years old.

"Call accepted," Baj said. "Hi Anda!"

Anda was calling from his home to find out about the kit of magical instruments that Baj had received. "Did you open it yet?" Anda asked even before his image emitted from the h-phone.

"I'm just opening it now. Want to see it?" Baj asked as he turned to the backpack on his bed.

"Yes!" Anda peered into his screen while he rotated his h-phone joystick to get a close up picture of Baj's backpack.

"Awwwwesommme!" Anda whispered as Baj unfurled the cape.

Baj was speechless as the cape waved and swirled in the air, almost as if it had a life of its own.

"Are the ear-clips in there?" Anda asked excitedly.

"Hold on. Let me check." Baj rummaged around in his backpack for a bit. He pulled out a laser pen, an Electrobuilder piece, and a clay impression of a matii leaf from an art project. There they were! He found the ear-clips. "Oh, here they are. And here's the Word Launcher too."

"Well? Are you going to let me see the cape on you?" asked Anda. "You promised that you would show me the cape."

Baj gulped and blinked his eyes while he stopped to think for a moment.

Chapter Two

The Box in Mr. Pilma's Office

Baj thought about the power of the instruments before him. He remembered Mr. Pilma's words when he called Baj into his office at school last month.

Mr. Pilma was the communication counselor at Baj's school. Baj met with Mr. Pilma three times a week after school. Mr. Pilma was helping Baj to use his words more appropriately, so Baj could match his words with his feelings and actions.

Sometimes Baj used the wrong words when he was mad or upset or just distracted by something else. Baj didn't mean to hurt anyone's feelings or anything. It was just that the words sometimes got all mixed up in his head when Baj got upset or distracted.

Mr. Pilma helped Baj straighten out his words and feelings. He taught Baj how to slow down his body and mind, so he could calm down and choose his words more carefully. Baj and Mr. Pilma talked together, or sometimes they played communication games or read books about listening better. But one day last month when Baj met with Mr. Pilma after school, he could tell that Mr. Pilma had something different planned for Baj.

Mr. Pilma's eyes were sparkling with excitement, and he could hardly contain the big grin that spread across his face. Baj knew that when someone was very smiley and quick moving that they were feeling excited.

"Do you notice something different?" Mr. Pilma asked Baj as he sat down at the table in Mr. Pilma's office. Baj knew that Mr. Pilma was quizzing him. He wanted to see if Baj could guess his emotion.

"Umm," Baj began, "you seem excited about something."

"That's right!" his teacher cried. "I *am* excited. Can you guess why?"

Baj looked around the room. Finally his eyes landed on the box on the table in front of Mr. Pilma. The box emitted an almost silent hum. Baj was pretty sure that Mr. Pilma was excited about the humming box, but he remembered to take a moment to think before he spoke. (Mr. Pilma had a gigantic poster on his wall that read: "STOP! LOOK! LISTEN! And THINK before you speak!" to help kids remember when the words got all mixed up in their heads.)

"Are you excited because of that box, Mr. Pilma?" Baj asked.

"Yes!" Mr. Pilma jumped up from his seat, and opened the humming box. "Good detective work, Baj." Baj smiled.

Carefully, Mr. Pilma pulled out the items from the box. A glorious cape waved in Mr. Pilma's hands as he set it on the table. Even after Mr. Pilma set down the cape, it continued to wave gently about the table. Next Mr. Pilma pulled out two curved black plastic pieces with tiny speakers that looked a lot like the earphones from Baj's wireless nano-disc music player. Last, he placed on the table a cool black pendant with a purple sparkling crystal at the throat.

Baj felt his heartbeat quicken. His breath seemed to get faster and shallower too. He felt a little hot and jittery. Baj was feeling nervous about the things from the box in Mr. Pilma's office.

"I feel nervous," Baj said, then paused to think some more. "And excited. And curious too."

"Appropriate feelings, Baj," Mr. Pilma said approvingly. "Take a deep breath and listen while I explain about these instruments."

At first Baj had trouble listening to Mr. Pilma's words. The nervous feelings made his mind feel all jumbly. Then he remembered some good "stop and think" words.

"Mr. Pilma," Baj said. "I need time to think about this for a minute."

Immediately, Mr. Pilma stopped talking and moving. "Good idea. I think I'll join you," said the teacher. Then Mr. Pilma sat back down and relaxed his shoulders. He closed his eyes and took deep belly breaths. Mr. Pilma made his belly slowly fill up with air by breathing in deeply through his nose. He held his breath for a moment, then he slowly let the air out through his mouth. Baj did the same. In no time at all, Baj felt his mind clear. His nervousness mostly went away, but his curiosity stayed.

"I'm ready to listen now," Baj told his teacher.

Slowly, Mr. Pilma explained that the instruments on the table were part of a Communication Clarifier Kit. (He also explained that the word clarifier came from the word clarify which meant to make something clearer or more easy to understand.) All three instruments in the kit worked together to help the user to communicate better with others. Mr. Pilma demonstrated how he could adjust the different instruments in the kit using its wireless control pad. The glowing labels on the pad had labels like "on/off," "decrease/increase," "visible/invisibility cloaking," and "sensory adjuster," but Mr. Pilma assured Baj that he wouldn't have to worry about using the control pad because it would stay in his office.

The purple crystal on the pendant was called a Word Launcher. It helped the user find the best words to match the situation. The earpieces were called Listening Aids, and they helped the user pick out the most important words coming into the user's ears. The cape, well, the cape was the most magnificent part of all. The cape was called a Calming Cape, and it was like putting on a warm, calming hug around the user's shoulders. The cape emitted gentle pulses into the user's body that made it easier to slow down, breathe, and think.

"The cape is sort of like my gigantic poster here," Mr. Pilma explained, pointing to the wall behind him. "The cape helps you remember to stop, look, listen and think. And plus," Mr. Pilma added with a smile, "the cape is just pretty darned cool too, don't you think?"

"Totally," Baj whispered in awe.

"Do you want to try it on?" the teacher asked.

"Uh sure," Baj stammered. "I mean no… actually, I'm not sure."

"Those are fine feelings to have," Mr. Pilma said. "You're not sure. You're feeling cautious. Tentative. Careful."

"Right. That's it," Baj said. "I think."

"Would you like to try just one piece on?" the teacher suggested. "Like maybe just the Listening Aids?"

"OK," Baj agreed. He felt relieved that Mr. Pilma wasn't making him try on the whole thing at once.

As Mr. Pilma fitted the earpieces around Baj's ears, he explained how the Listening Aids worked.

"Now Baj, you'll hear things exactly the way you normally would, except you might hear some extra stuff too. For instance, some words might seem louder or be repeated by the machine. Those are the important words that someone is saying."

Baj breathed deeply as Mr. Pilma spoke. It seemed like just being near the Calming Cape made Baj feel more relaxed.

"The other neat thing about the Listening Aids is the extra words they let you hear. Like if your mom or dad is asking you to do something that you might not want to do, but that you have to do…"

"Like clean my room?" Baj asked.

"That's right," the teacher smiled. "Like clean your room. The Listening Aids, will tell you when and why something is a 'Have-To'."

"A Have-To?" Baj asked.

"Yeah, I think we talked about Have-To's a couple weeks ago," Mr. Pilma said. "A Have-To is something you *have to* do, like cleaning your room. A 'Choose-To' is something you can *choose to* do or not, like playing by yourself or playing with a friend at recess."

"I think I understand," Baj said.

"I'm here to help you with the instruments, Baj," Mr. Pilma reassured him. "Just ask me any questions when you get confused."

"Can you write down how the instruments in the Communication Clarifier Kit work?" asked Baj softly.

"Of course!" Mr. Pilma answered loudly. "Why didn't I think of that? What a great suggestion! Writing things down *always* helps you to remember important stuff." Mr. Pilma rummaged around among the machinery on the table.

"Here it is! Here are the instructions that go with the Communication Clarifier Kit. That way, if you forget how something works, you can just look it up in this booklet." Mr. Pilma handed him the electronic instruction booklet. Baj put it in his backpack right away, so he wouldn't forget it.

Then Mr. Pilma adjusted the earpieces so they fitted snugly around Baj's ears. They felt so light that he could hardly tell they were there. Mr. Pilma pressed a button on the wireless control pad on the table.

"OK, Baj," Mr. Pilma said. "The Listening Aids are now on."

Listening Aids on, were the words Baj heard softly repeated in his earpieces. Those were the important words.

"It feels sort of strange," Baj said. "But I think I'll get used to it."

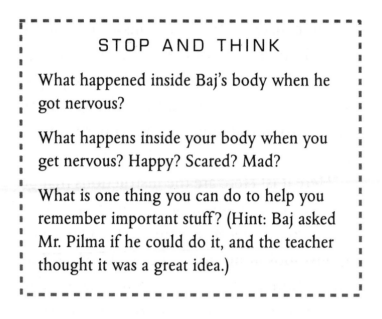

STOP AND THINK

What happened inside Baj's body when he got nervous?

What happens inside your body when you get nervous? Happy? Scared? Mad?

What is one thing you can do to help you remember important stuff? (Hint: Baj asked Mr. Pilma if he could do it, and the teacher thought it was a great idea.)

"Let's just do something regular, like playing that card game I taught you called Duo," Mr. Pilma suggested.

"No, I don't want to," Baj said. Something was making him feel jumbly inside.

"How about Old Magnateen?" Mr. Pilma tried to suggest another game.

"No. Nothing," Baj said. The jumbly feeling stayed.

"OK. You choose the game, Baj," the teacher said. And Baj heard the words: **He just wants to play a game with you.**

"Do you just want to play a game with me?" Baj asked.

"Yes," the teacher answered. "That's right."

The Listening Aids said: **Tell him if you want to play too.**

"I want to play too," Baj said.

"I was wondering if you wanted to play," Mr. Pilma said. "You kept saying no."

He wants to know why you were saying no.

"I was feeling weird with the Listening Aids on," Baj said. "I feel better now. Let's play Duo."

Mr. Pilma and Baj played Duo for ten minutes, but it was an unlucky day for Baj. He started to feel his shoulders bunch up. Instead of saying the words, he spat them and his voice became hard and short, like a spike. His head hung down and his face frowned. Baj was upset, grouchy and mad. His mind became jumbly.

"OK, Baj," Mr. Pilma said, flipping down a card. "Draw four."

This is just a card game, the Listening Aids reminded him.

Baj became more upset. He didn't want to take four more cards. He was holding four cards already, and four more would make eight cards altogether. Baj was worried that he might not be able to hold all eight cards in his hand without dropping some.

Finally, Baj became too frustrated. He threw down his cards on the table. Some cards even fell on the floor. Baj felt like screaming and kicking. He also felt like crying. Baj had lost his temper. Mr. Pilma frowned. Baj felt terrible.

"Tell me what you are feeling, Baj," Mr. Pilma asked.

What are you feeling? asked the Listening Aids.

"Go away! I hate you!" Baj shouted at Mr. Pilma. He was very upset now. Completely jumbly in his brain. He had lost control of his words. It felt like all the wrong words were bubbling around in Baj's head.

The Listening Aids were programmed to help Baj remember the right words: **You are good. Your words were bad.**

Mr. Pilma was frowning harder now. His arms were crossed over his chest and he turned his face away from Baj.

Your words hurt the teacher's feelings.

Baj felt terrible about hurting Mr. Pilma's feelings, but he was still so upset about the game. Baj was kicking the table hard, so the cards were bouncing all over the place and spilling onto the floor. Baj didn't know how to fix the situation, and that made him feel even worse.

Fix it, the Listening Aids urged him.

Baj kicked the table over and over. The cards were skittering all across the table. Mr. Pilma was still frowning. He turned his chair all the way round, so his back was to Baj.

You can fix this, the Listening Aids echoed.

Baj began to cry as he gave the table one last hard kick that sent the Calming Cape sliding across the table and onto his lap.

Stop. Breathe. Think. The Listening Aids voiced the intent of the Calming Cape.

Baj relaxed his body and breathed. He felt some of the mad feeling go away, but he still felt very bad about the words he had flung at Mr. Pilma. He remembered the words of the Listening Aids: **You can fix this.**

"I don't know how to fix this problem," Baj finally said aloud. His mind still felt jumbly. The right words felt very, very far away.

STOP AND THINK

What words could Baj use to fix the situation?

How can Baj make his mind feel less jumbly?

"Think about the words you said to me," Mr. Pilma said, still facing in the opposite direction.

Think of words: Hate. Go away.

Baj frowned. His shoulders drooped and he felt tears stinging his eyes. He felt sad and ashamed. He didn't want to tell Mr. Pilma the mean words he had used and he wished he'd never said those words at all. Baj wished he had stopped and thought for a moment about why he was upset rather than yelling at Mr. Pilma. But Baj knew he had to answer. He knew that if he didn't answer then Mr. Pilma would just get more hurt and upset with Baj.

"I told you that I hate you. Now you don't like me," Baj said, his head falling to his chest. The tears came down his cheeks. Baj still felt very sad and ashamed.

"I still like you, Baj," Mr. Pilma said. "I just don't like your words."

You are good. Words were bad, the Listening Aids said. **Fix it.**

"I can't think of any words to fix it!" The Calming Cape fell to the floor. Baj felt sad and bad flood over his brain.

"I'll give you time to think of fixing words," Mr. Pilma said.

Baj bent down to pick up the Calming Cape. He felt big breaths fill his lungs. He allowed his mind to think, what two words could fix this problem? Baj's mind cleared as the words appeared in his brain.

"I'm sorry," Baj said to his teacher. Mr. Pilma turned around to face Baj. He was smiling a little.

He forgives you. Keep talking.

"I got, uh, frustrated with the game. I wasn't winning, and I felt mad." The words were flowing out of Baj's mouth. "I felt mad. I forgot that it was just a game. I said some things that I should not have said, and now I feel bad. I'm sorry, Mr. Pilma. I'm really sorry."

Mr. Pilma was really smiling now.

Yes! the Listening Aids said. **You fixed it!**

"Thank you for the apology, Baj," the teacher said.

"Do you want to keep playing the card game?" Baj asked.

"I'm sorry, but our time is up," Mr. Pilma said. "It's time for you to go home."

Time is up.

"I don't want to leave," Baj frowned.

"I understand," Mr. Pilma said.

Time to go now. It's a Have-To.

"Is this a Have-To?" Baj asked.

"Yes, it is."

"OK," Baj said.

"I'll see you the day after tomorrow," the teacher reminded him.

Play again later.

"OK." Baj turned to leave.

"Oh, Baj," Mr. Pilma said. "You're still wearing the Listening Aids."

He might want you to give them back.

"Do I have to give them back? Can I keep them?" Baj asked.

"Sure," the teacher answered. "You can wear the cape too, if you want."

"No, that's OK." Baj put the cape on the table. "I'll just try the Listening Aids for now."

"Sounds fine to me. I'll leave the Listening Aids activated." Mr. Pilma pushed some buttons on the Communication Clarifier Kit control panel. "See you on Wednesday."

"Bye!" Baj said as he ran out the door. And then he added, "Thanks for your help today."

Mr. Pilma smiled broadly.

STOP AND THINK

Why did Baj throw the cards?

What would you have done if you were losing the game?

What were the bad words Baj said to his teacher?

What words could he have said instead?

Can you think of some fixing words?

Chapter Three

It's a Have-To

Baj was playing with his Electrobuilders in the family room. He was in the middle of building a replica of the moon shuttle that he and his family had flown in during a recent visit to Aular's Zeta Moon.

"Baj! It's dinnertime," his mom called out. "Please go wash your hands."

Go wash hands, his Listening Aids echoed softly.

Baj didn't listen, though. He was concentrating on a really tricky part of the launching pad. His newest Electrobuilder set came with an air burst release valve that made the moon shuttle actually shoot up from the launching pad. Baj was having some trouble figuring out how to hook it up. His brows were knit together in a hard bunch, his mouth was set in a tight, short line and his shoulders were hunched around his ears.

However, Baj wasn't the only one in the family becoming frustrated at that moment. "Baj! Did you hear me?" His mom's voice was louder and sterner now.

The Listening Aids were louder too: **Stop playing. Wash hands!**

"I don't want to!" Baj called back to his mom.

Soon, he saw his mom's feet standing near the launching pad. She was frowning. Her arms were crossed. Her forehead was all wrinkled. She wasn't happy.

"You don't look happy," Baj said, looking up.

"No, I am not happy," his mother said.

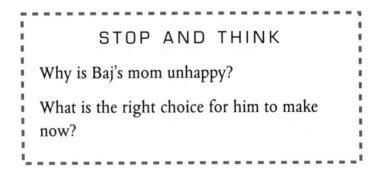

STOP AND THINK

Why is Baj's mom unhappy?

What is the right choice for him to make now?

Baj felt a little confused. He wasn't sure why his mom felt unhappy, so he did something Mr. Pilma had taught him to do when he wasn't sure what someone was feeling: he asked her.

"Why are you upset, Mom?"

"I am upset, Baj, because you ignored me when I asked you to wash up," his mother explained. "I decided to make dinner *without* using the RoboChef tonight. I have been working for the last *hour* in the kitchen to get dinner on the table, and I don't want it to get cold."

She doesn't like being ignored. Fix it.

Baj smiled a little. He knew how to fix it. "I'm sorry I ignored you, Mom."

His mom's forehead became smooth, her shoulders relaxed and she smiled a little. "Thanks for saying that, Baj."

Baj smiled back at his mom. He felt good that he could fix the problem. He started playing with the Electrobuilders again. The shuttle needed a few more lights.

"Baj," his mom said, "aren't you forgetting something?"

She wants you to wash your hands.

"I don't want to wash up, Mom!" Baj whined.

"Baj…" his mom warned him in a deep growl.

The Listening Aids explained, **This is a Have-To.**

"Do I have to?" Baj checked, just in case the Listening Aids were wrong.

"Yes," his mom said. "Dinner is ready, and everybody is sitting at the table waiting for you."

Go now.

"OK." Baj jumped up and rushed to the bathroom. He didn't like to stop playing, but his mom said he had to. Sometimes when an adult, especially a parent or teacher, says you have to do something, you just have to – unless they are telling you to do something that you know is really wrong or bad or will hurt someone. That's part of being a kid: listening to directions.

Even though Baj still wanted to play, he felt good at using words to make his mom happy.

Besides, he could always play with his Electro-builders after dinner. And he did.

STOP AND THINK

What made Baj's mom mad?

Why did Baj have to wash his hands?

What does a "Have-To" mean?

Chapter Four

The Race of the StarCruiser Ultimate XR

Baj imagined that his flying bicycle was a StarCruiser Ultimate XR, the fastest solo space jet in the galaxy. Baj swerved and swooped as he flew along the cycle lane, pretending that he was racing to the planet Neri instead of just flying to school. Baj didn't hear his best friend Anda whiz up beside him.

"Hey, Bajimoto," Anda called out happily. Anda and Baj thought it was really funny to make up wacky names for each other.

The Listening Aids did not realize that Anda was talking to Baj. They remained silent.

"Hellooo?" Anda called again. "Bajarelli? You in there?"

In Baj's mind he was racing against the clock as his StarCruiser Ultimate XR sped at light speed toward Neri. Baj was so involved in his imagined race that he hadn't even heard his friend calling him.

Meanwhile, Anda was beginning to feel hurt. He thought Baj was ignoring him on purpose. Anda frowned quietly, his pedaling slowed down and his head hung low. He tried talking to his friend one last time.

"Are...are you mad at me, Baj?" Anda asked sadly.

Mad at friend? The Listening Aids finally spoke up when they detected Baj's name.

"Oh!" Baj eventually noticed his friend Anda. He slowed his flying bicycle to match the speed of Anda's flying bike. "Did you say something?"

Anda huffed and turned away from Baj. He slowed his flying bike still further so that Baj had to shift into low speed just to stay with him.

Friend upset, the Listening Aids suggested.

Baj was very confused. He couldn't figure out why Anda would be upset with him. Baj remembered Mr. Pilma's advice: *When in doubt, ask.*

"Anda, what's the matter?" Baj asked.

Anda remained silent. Anda's feelings were hurt because he thought Baj had been ignoring him on purpose. Anda felt like riding away from Baj.

STOP AND THINK

Why are Anda's feelings hurt?

Did Baj hurt Anda on purpose?

What should Anda do now?

What should Baj do now?

Baj tried to read his friend's body language. Mr. Pilma had taught Baj all about how people can talk without saying anything at all. They used their bodies to communicate. It was called "body language."

Baj noticed that Anda's mouth was turned down, and his forehead was wrinkled. Anda's shoulders were raised up, and his head was lowered. In fact, Anda's whole body looked sort of like a deflated balloon, all limp and droopy.

"Are you sad, Anda?" Baj finally asked.

Anda sighed. "Yes, I'm sad!" he finally cried. "I was trying to say hi to you, and you didn't even answer me!"

Friend hurt, ignored, the Listening Aids echoed quietly in Baj's ear. **You can fix this.**

"I'm sorry, Anda," Baj said. He told Anda the truth. "I didn't even hear you."

"How could you not hear me?" Anda shouted. He seemed to be angry too. "I was talking right to you."

"I guess I was sort of stuck in my imagination," Baj explained.

"Oh," Anda answered.

You told the truth. You fixed it.

"Do you accept my apology?" Baj asked his buddy.

"Of course I do," Anda answered. Then Anda added some very important advice. "But next time, you should keep one ear and one eye open for what's going on around you, even when you are imagining things."

Keep an eye and an ear open at all times.

"Thanks, Anda. I'll try to remember that." Baj smiled at his friend. Anda smiled back. Mr. Pilma always said that smiles were catchy. If you smiled at someone, they would probably smile back. Frowns were catchy too, though, and Baj had to be careful about that.

"Hey, Anda!" Baj's smile shone brighter. "Want to join me in my imagination?"

Anda raised an eyebrow and shrugged his shoulders.

Friend interested. Go on, said the Listening Aids.

"I was pretending that I was on StarCruiser Ultimate XR racing at light speed to Neri," Baj explained with excitement in his voice.

Anda's eyes got round and his face seemed to light up. He shifted his flying bike to high speed, and sat up high in his seat.

Friend wants to play.

"Want to play?" Baj asked, speeding up his bike.

"Only if I get to ride the SpaceSpeeder 45 with mega rocket boosters," Anda gushed as he brought his flying bike into a spectacular swoop.

"Cool!" Baj said. "Let's go!"

Baj and Anda raced all the way to school. Their flying bicycles swerved and swooped all over their lanes. They were laughing pretty hard by the time they swooshed into the school's gravitational field.

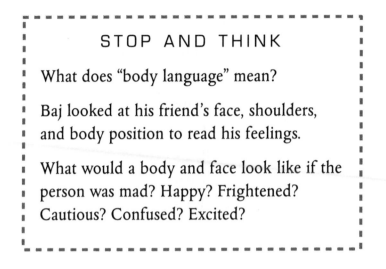

STOP AND THINK

What does "body language" mean?

Baj looked at his friend's face, shoulders, and body position to read his feelings.

What would a body and face look like if the person was mad? Happy? Frightened? Cautious? Confused? Excited?

Chapter Five

A Problem Solved

It was Wednesday afternoon and Baj was knocking on Mr. Pilma's office door and waiting for an answer. When nobody responded, Baj knocked again, a little louder. Still no answer. Baj was puzzled and a little worried. He sensed the jumbly feeling starting inside his body.

Baj wasn't sure what to do next. Usually, Mr. Pilma answered the door right away. Maybe, Baj thought, he should just go ahead and open the door. What if Mr. Pilma had forgotten about him? What if he was supposed to just go home? What if Mr. Pilma was hurt? What if he never saw his teacher again? Baj's scary thoughts made his heart beat faster. His shoulders bunched up, and his body felt hot and sweaty. Baj was worried, nervous, and anxious.

"What shall I do?" Baj asked himself. It was then that he remembered the gigantic poster in Mr. Pilma's office. Baj stopped, looked, listened, and thought. But his mind was still too jumbly to make the words and feelings clear again.

STOP AND THINK

What should Baj do to calm himself down?

What should he do after his mind clears?

Baj took a deep belly breath in through his nose, and slowly let the air seep out through his mouth. He took another deep breath and another. He thought about a happy memory: he and Anda riding their flying bikes to school, pretending to be racing StarCruisers.

Soon Baj's body looked and felt calmer. His shoulders released back down to their usual position. His jaw wasn't tightened up and the muscles in his face were relaxed. He almost felt like he could fall asleep. Baj was pleased to notice that his mind became clearer when his body relaxed.

Baj decided to sit outside Mr. Pilma's office door and wait for him. Then he decided that if Mr. Pilma hadn't arrived in ten minutes – Baj looked at his watch, it was 3:15pm now – he would go to the office and explain the problem to the school secretary. Usually the school secretary could solve any problem. Baj smiled, relieved that he had made a good decision.

Only 3 minutes and 15 seconds later, Baj looked up to see Mr. Pilma rushing down the hallway. "Hi Baj," Mr. Pilma said, huffing and puffing. "Sorry I'm late."

Teacher was late, said the Listening Aids.

"I was worried about you," Baj said.

"I'm glad that you told me that, Baj," Mr. Pilma said. "I'm sorry that I worried you."

He's sorry.

"Is everything OK?" Baj asked. "I was worried that something bad might have happened."

"Everything is fine, Baj," Mr. Pilma smiled warmly. "I had to fly my daughter to her basketball practice. Her flying scooter is in the repair port."

Daughter needed a ride.

"Oh, OK," Baj said as he followed his teacher into the office. "Basketball? Oh yeah, that's an Earthling game, right?"

"Uh, yes it is," Mr. Pilma responded as he entered his office. "So tell me Baj, how has it been going with the Listening Aids?"

"Pretty well," Baj answered. He paused until Mr. Pilma took a seat. When he looked Baj in the eyes, Baj knew that Mr. Pilma was ready to listen, so he continued.

Baj told him how the Listening Aids had helped him understand that people don't like to be ignored when they're talking to you, like when his mom was asking him to wash up for dinner or when Anda was calling to him on the way to school. He had also learned that some things are a Have-To, and that means that he just has to do it without complaining.

Baj was talking very quickly, and his arms were waving all around as he spoke. His face seemed bright. He was excited about the Listening Aids.

"And yesterday," Baj was saying, "Ms. Rrocey, my teacher, asked the whole class to clean up after free choice time, and the Listening Aids reminded me that when a teacher gives instructions it's a Have-To."

"That's true," Mr. Pilma nodded and smiled. He seemed pleased.

"And guess what?" Baj asked. "I was the first one to clean up!"

"Wow, Baj!" exclaimed Mr. Pilma. "Congratulations!"

"Wait, it gets better," Baj continued in an enthusiastic voice. "I noticed that my classmate Aima was having trouble picking up all the Electrobuilders that she had played with, so I helped her clean them up! Without even being asked!"

"Terrific, Baj," Mr. Pilma said grinning. "Did the Listening Aids tell you to help her?"

"Actually, no. They didn't," answered Baj. "I just stopped, looked around the classroom, listened to the kids, and thought about what to do next, and that's when I noticed that she needed help."

"How did you feel after you helped Aima?" asked Mr. Pilma.

"It felt really good," Baj answered. "Aima even said thank you, and later that day she asked if she could play with me at recess!"

Mr. Pilma just sat back in his chair and smiled broadly. His body looked relaxed, and he seemed happy, but he didn't say anything.

"You look proud of me, Mr. Pilma," Baj guessed.

Mr. Pilma clapped his hands and laughed. "Yes, Baj," he said. "I am very, very proud of you."

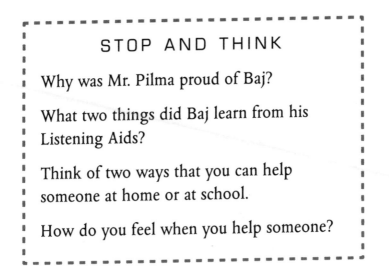

STOP AND THINK

Why was Mr. Pilma proud of Baj?

What two things did Baj learn from his Listening Aids?

Think of two ways that you can help someone at home or at school.

How do you feel when you help someone?

Chapter Six

The Calming Cape

After they had talked for a while, Baj and Mr. Pilma played a quick game of Duo. Once again, luck was against Baj, and he lost the game.

It's only a game, the Listening Aids reminded him.

"You're frowning, Baj," Mr. Pilma observed. "I wonder if you are starting to feel frustrated that you're not winning today."

Baj thought for a moment before answering. "Yes, I am getting frustrated," he finally said. "I don't like to lose, I guess."

"Maybe this would be a good time to try on the Calming Cape," Mr. Pilma suggested.

Try on Calming Cape, the Listening Aids echoed softly.

"Hmmm," Baj thought, "I'm not so sure about that cape."

"What are you feeling?" Mr. Pilma asked. Baj thought that "What are you feeling?" must be Mr. Pilma's favorite question!

Baj took a deep breath. "When I think about wearing the cape I feel nervous and, uh, weird and, um, um, kind of embarrassed, I guess."

"I understand the nervous and weird feelings," Mr. Pilma said, "but I don't see what the embarrassed feeling is all about."

Why embarrassed?

"I am embarrassed because," Baj started slowly, then quickly shot out the rest of his thought, "because of what the other kids might think when they see me wearing a cape in school."

Though Baj's face felt hot and flushed, he still felt much better as soon as the words were out of his mouth. Mr. Pilma seemed to understand this.

"Oh, I see," Mr. Pilma said. "Thank you for telling me how you feel. Now I understand. And now that I understand, I can help you solve this problem."

Baj looked at Mr. Pilma's face. His forehead was not wrinkled. His shoulders were down and he had a small smile on his face. He didn't seem unhappy or disappointed.

"Maybe I could just wear the cape at home," Baj offered. The truth was that Baj really wanted to try out that magical-looking cape. He was just worried that his friends would ask him too many questions about it, or maybe they would feel jealous that they didn't have a cape like that. Baj was pretty sure that Mr. Pilma didn't have enough capes for everyone in his class.

"I think I might have a solution to this problem," Mr. Pilma said at last. He began pushing buttons on the Communication Clarifier Kit control panel. Baj felt relieved that Mr. Pilma could fix the problem. "Yes, here it is," Mr. Pilma said as he pushed one last button.

There was a slight buzzing noise and Baj watched in amazement as the Calming Cape disappeared from the table.

"Whoa! How did you do that?" Baj wondered out loud. "Where did it go?"

"It's right there, Baj," Mr. Pilma said smiling. "Feel it."

Baj carefully put out his hand. He could feel the gentle waves and reassuring pulses of the Calming Cape, but he couldn't see anything at all. He couldn't believe his eyes – or rather, his fingers! Baj's eyes were wide. His mouth fell open and he couldn't speak. He was shocked, surprised, and amazed.

Mr. Pilma chuckled. "It's not magic, Baj. I just programmed the cape to utilize its invisibility shield. Now you can wear it without anyone even knowing it."

The cape can be invisible.

"Wow," Baj said. "Can it reappear?"

"Sure," the teacher answered. "There are two ways to make it visible. I can push this button here," Mr. Pilma pointed to a blinking blue button on the control panel that read "Cape Visibility Shield." "Or the user – that's you – just squeezes a corner of the cape while giving the 'Shield on' or 'Shield off' command."

With Baj's OK, Mr. Pilma velcroed the Calming Cape around Baj's neck. Baj practiced squeezing the cape and commanding it to disappear and reappear. Finally he said with a smile, "I like this cape."

"I thought you might." Mr. Pilma was smiley too. (*Smiles are catchy!*) "Just remember Baj, the cape will help you remember to stop and think or to breathe deep belly breaths, or do whatever you need to do to keep the words from getting jumbly."

"So I'll never be mad or sad again?" Baj asked hopefully.

"Not exactly," Mr. Pilma explained. "You will still feel all the natural feelings – sad, mad, scared, upset, happy, surprised, excited, and so on – but the Calming Cape will help you remember how to keep your mind clear."

Baj's body slumped and his face looked sad. He was disappointed. "I wish I never had to feel bad feelings again."

"I know what you mean, Baj," Mr. Pilma said, "but those are important feelings to have. For one thing, they keep our bodies safe."

"Really?" Baj asked.

"Sure," Mr. Pilma said, nodding his head. "When your body is feeling scared of something, it's warning you to be careful."

"Like when I'm flying my bike too fast," Baj asked, "and I get a jumpy feeling inside my chest? Is that my body warning me to slow down?"

"That's right," his teacher said with a grin. "Or when there is a fire, and you get scared. Or when someone is mean to you, and you get mad."

"The mad makes me want to stay away from the mean person."

"Exactly right, Baj," the teacher said, nodding and smiling even more.

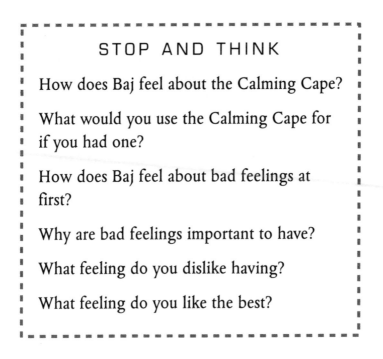

STOP AND THINK

How does Baj feel about the Calming Cape?

What would you use the Calming Cape for if you had one?

How does Baj feel about bad feelings at first?

Why are bad feelings important to have?

What feeling do you dislike having?

What feeling do you like the best?

Chapter Seven

The "Super Risa" Solution

As soon as Baj landed in the suspended garage outside his house, he activated the Calming Cape with a quick squeeze and quiet command to turn shields off. All at once, his cape appeared in fabulous waves of ever-changing colors and hues. Not only did it feel like a gentle hug around Baj's shoulders, but it looked like a gentle hug, if that was possible.

"Holy moly," whispered his little sister Risa when she saw him walk in the door. "What a cool cape."

She likes cape, the Listening Aids said.

"Thanks," Baj replied as he headed up to his bedroom. "Mr. Pilma gave it to me."

"Does it help you listen like the earpieces?" Risa asked, tagging along behind him. The whole family was excited about Baj's new Communication Clarifier Kit. They asked about it at dinner almost every night.

"No," Baj said. "It's a Calming Cape. It helps me clear my mind, so my words and feelings don't get all mixed up." Baj plopped his backpack on the floor, and turned to look at his sister.

"You are so lucky, Baji," gushed Risa. "Can I try it on?"

Sister wants to try it. She wishes she had a cape too.

"Hmmm," Baj put his hand to his chin. "Let me think about it for a minute."

Risa was pleasantly surprised. Usually Baj would say no without even thinking about it. Risa knew that if she let Baj think quietly for a minute then he would probably make a good decision.

"Mr. Pilma said that I wasn't supposed to be careless with the cape," Baj said slowly.

Immediately, Risa jumped in, "I'll be really, really careful, Baji. I promise!"

Baj took another moment to think. He looked at his sister. Though sometimes Risa could be sort of pesky, most of the time she was lots of fun. In fact, Risa was one of Baj's favorite people to play with. And most of all, she was a careful person, well, most of the time.

"OK," Baj agreed as he released the Calming Cape from around his neck. He chuckled as Risa jumped up and down, clapping her hands. She was happy and excited.

"Thanks, Baji!" Risa squealed.

Sister happy, the Listening Aids whispered. "No kidding," thought Baj. Most of the time, Risa's body language was very easy to read.

With the cape over her shoulders, Risa ran around the room. She jumped on and off the bed, pretending she was a flying superhero. "Super Risa to the rescue!" Baj's sister hollered as she catapulted about the room.

Risa and Baj spent the next 20 minutes playing superheroes. They were laughing as they jumped all around his bedroom. Baj was very happy that he had decided to share the Calming Cape with Risa. He felt good in his heart when he saw his sister enjoying the cape so much.

After a while, Baj started to feel tired of playing. It had been a long day at school, and he needed some time to himself. He knew that if he didn't have some quiet time alone in his room after school, then he would start feeling grouchy. Risa knew about Baj's after school quiet time too, but sometimes she forgot. This was one of those times.

"OK, Risa," Baj said. "Time to give me back my cape now."

Risa kept jumping on Baj's bed. She didn't answer him.

"OK, Risa," Baj repeated louder. "Time to take off the cape."

"Super Risa!" his sister yelled. She ran out of Baj's room with the Calming Cape flying elegantly behind her.

She does not want to stop playing, the Listening Aid said.

"I *know* that!" Baj muttered as he trailed his sister into the family room. Baj was tired, hungry, and almost out of patience. He also was starting to worry that Risa would never, ever give back the Calming Cape. What if she never gave it back? What would Mr. Pilma do if Risa lost the cape? What if Baj could never stop Risa from wearing the cape, ever, ever, ever???

Baj's body felt tight. His face scowled and his breathing got faster. He clenched his fists. Baj was feeling angry and frustrated with his sister.

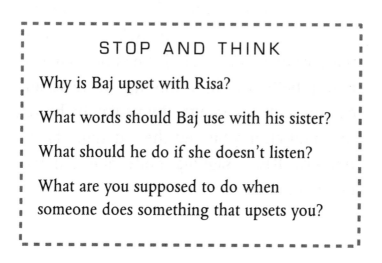

STOP AND THINK

Why is Baj upset with Risa?

What words should Baj use with his sister?

What should he do if she doesn't listen?

What are you supposed to do when someone does something that upsets you?

"RISA! STOP IT!" Baj exploded.

The smile faded from Risa's face. The Calming Cape drooped from her shoulders.

"Give me back my cape *now!*" Baj yelled. No thoughts went through Baj's head except for red anger at his sister.

Risa immediately stopped in her tracks. She realized that Baj had been pushed too far. He had lost his temper and now he was mad at her. She worried that he would never let her use the cape again.

"Sorry, Baj," Risa said in a small voice. Her body became small and floppy too. She felt bad. Risa handed him back his cape.

Baj put on the Calming Cape. Embracing its user's shoulders, the Calming Cape seemed to come to life, wrapping itself around Baj's body. At that moment, Baj remembered to take a deep belly breath, in through his nose, and out through his mouth. Immediately, he felt his mind clear a bit and the red anger faded. Baj saw Risa's sagging body and sad face before him.

"Sorry I lost my temper," Baj explained, still feeling a little mad, "but you weren't listening to me."

"I'm sorry too," Risa apologized back, and Baj was amazed anew at the power of the words "I'm sorry."

Then Risa pushed her luck a little more. "But can I wear the cape again after dinner? Please?"

She just wants to borrow it, the Listening Aids explained.

"Hmmm," Baj mused. He wanted to say no right away, but instead he said, "Let me think." On one hand, Baj was worried that if he let Risa borrow the cape she might not give it back when he asked. On the other hand, he wanted to be a nice brother and friend.

"Please! Please! Please!" Risa begged. "I promise that I'll give it right back when you ask."

She will give back the cape.

"Well, maybe. We'll try just one more time," Baj agreed. "But if you don't give it back when

I ask *the first time,* then you can't use it again for a really long time."

"It's a deal," Risa nodded her head enthusiastically.

Both Risa and Baj were smiling now. They had worked it out. The Calming Cape had helped Baj to regain his cool, so his mind could work clearly. Baj and Risa had talked calmly and had come to an agreement. They each went to their separate rooms feeling like they were both winners.

Chapter Eight

The Word Launcher

A week later, Baj and Mr. Pilma were playing Duo again. Baj was wearing his Calming Cape and his Listening Aids.

"Something is different about the Listening Aids lately, Mr. Pilma," Baj explained as he set down a purple-striped dragon card on the table.

"What is it?" asked Mr. Pilma.

"They don't talk to me as much," Baj said. His eyebrows were pushed way up on his forehead and his eyes were wide. Even his voice felt a little quaky. Baj was nervous that he had broken the Listening Aids, and that Mr. Pilma would be mad. He was surprised and confused to see Mr. Pilma lean back in his chair with a little grin on his face.

"You're not mad?" Baj asked.

"No, I'm not mad," Mr. Pilma assured him. "Do I look mad?"

"Well, no, I guess not."

"Actually Baj, I am happy."

"You are?"

"Yes," the teacher said. "The Listening Aids are programmed to decrease their activity when you don't need them as much."

Baj must have looked confused because Mr. Pilma continued to explain. "The Listening Aids aren't talking to you as much because you are getting better at understanding what people are trying to tell you."

"I am?" Baj asked, smiling.

"Yes. You are improving at listening," Mr. Pilma went on, "and I think you are remembering to breathe, stop, and think more and more too."

"Wow," Baj exhaled.

Mr. Pilma laughed. Then he asked his famous question, "How does that make you feel, Baj?"

Baj thought for a moment. "I feel happy... and surprised...and most of all, really proud."

Mr. Pilma smiled more broadly. "It seems to me, Baj, that you are ready to try out the Word Launcher."

"I was hoping you would say that," Baj said.

Mr. Pilma laughed again. Baj suspected that Mr. Pilma was proud of him. But then Mr. Pilma's face became more serious as he took the Word Launcher from its box. Baj could see that the Word Launcher looked like a shimmering, magical pendant hanging from a very thin, black string. The Word Launcher changed from shimmering purple to a prism-slike quality that made it look like no color and every color at the same time. It seemed to actually emit a faint glow, like a pulsating rainbow, changing colors slightly with every beat.

Though the Word Launcher looked exciting, Mr. Pilma's face told Baj that using the tools in the Communication Clarifier Kit was serious business.

"The Word Launcher will help you find the best possible words for the situation," Mr. Pilma explained. "For instance, did you know,

Baj, that sometimes you get so worried about something that you use *extreme words*?"

"Extreme words?" Baj questioned his teacher.

Mr. Pilma answered, "Let me give you some examples of extreme words: always, never, forever, the most, the least, hate…"

"Oh," Baj felt as if a lightbulb had gone on in his head, "like when I get mad at my sister Risa and say that she can *never* play with me again?"

"Right," the teacher agreed. "You use those words because you are so mad at that moment, but really…"

"Really I will play with her again, of course," Baj interrupted, "just not for a while."

"Or sometimes you feel worried that the worst will happen," Mr. Pilma said gravely.

Baj nodded. His face mirrored the teacher's serious expression. "Like when I thought you would *never* come to our meeting last week?"

"Oh yeah," Mr. Pilma remembered, "that time I was late."

"I thought you would never come," Baj repeated. "I thought that I would never see you again."

"But really you were *worried* that would happen," Mr. Pilma said. "Baj, do you think that I would really just leave you forever like that? Just waiting alone in the hallway?"

"Uh, no," Baj admitted. "I guess not. I guess I was just nervous that would happen."

"You were scared that I would never get there that day, but deep down you knew that I would be there eventually, right?"

"Even if you did miss our meeting," Baj figured out loud, "things would work out. I wouldn't sit in the hallway forever."

Mr. Pilma cracked a smile. "Of course you wouldn't have!"

"I think I'm ready to try on the Word Launcher now," Baj said, his eyes fixed on the shimmering crystal the teacher was holding.

Quickly, Mr. Pilma stood up and came around the table. He reached around Baj's neck to secure the Word Launcher firmly in place.

"It's official," said Mr. Pilma solemnly. "Now you have the whole Communication Clarifier Kit working: the Word Launcher, the Calming Cape, and the Listening Aids."

"Wow," replied Baj.

"What do you say we take this show on the road?" Mr. Pilma asked with one hand on the doorknob.

Baj wasn't sure what Mr. Pilma meant when he said that, but when he started to open the door and headed out, Baj figured that he wanted him to follow.

"Where are we going?" Baj asked.

"Let's try out the Word Launcher with the After School crowd," explained Mr. Pilma.

"Sure!" said Baj. "My friend Ttywa is in After School."

Baj and Mr. Pilma walked out to the school playground. Baj felt his heart racing a bit, and he was breathing sort of fast. He was nervous about trying out the whole Communication Clarifier Kit all at once, but fortunately the Calming Cape, with its invisibility shield on, was hugging his shoulders, reminding him to breathe deeply from his belly. As a result, Baj's mind stayed clear. He was surprised and delighted that he could be nervous and clear-headed at the same time. He felt his shoulders push back and his chest stand out. His chin lifted slightly, and he smiled a little.

Baj was proud of himself. And he had reason to be proud: being nervous and clear-headed is very hard for any person to be.

STOP AND THINK

Why was Baj proud of himself?

How had he kept his mind clear even though he was nervous?

What makes you feel proud?

Suddenly, out of nowhere, a group of fifth-graders slammed into Baj's body. The bigger kids had been playing gravity-free whiz ball, and Baj had accidentally wandered onto the whiz ball court. The boys hadn't noticed him there, and they knocked him down as they went for the orbiting ball.

Baj fell to the ground and scraped his hands. Blood rushed painfully to the palm of his right hand and to his ears as well. In fact, Baj felt all sorts of bad feelings flooding into his head. He was hurt, and he was also mad, really mad, upset, and kind of embarrassed that the boys had hurt him. At that moment, Baj felt certain that those dumb boys had knocked him down on purpose. Baj felt so angry that he felt like hitting those fifth-grade meanies.

Baj started to raise his arm to swing his fist at the boys, but he found that he couldn't move it from his side. The Calming Cape gently held it down.

"Are you OK, buddy?" one of the fifth graders asked.

"Oh geez!" another boy exclaimed, "I am *so sorry!*"

"Sorry, Baj," said a boy who Baj recognized as his best friend Anda's older brother Liiwal. "It was an accident."

All of the fifth-grade kids on the court spoke at once. Baj's mind started to whirl. But then he heard a clear, firm voice inside his ear.

It was an accident.

They didn't mean to hurt you.

The boys are very sorry.

Baj took a deep breath. His right hand had begun to throb badly now, and he was still quite upset. He wanted to yell at those kids. He still suspected that they had meant to hurt him. Maybe they had knocked him down on purpose.

Baj tried to yell at them. He wanted to shout, "I hate you! You *always* try to hurt me! I'm *never* going to feel better. *Ever!*" But the Word Launcher tightened just a little bit around his throat, holding the words inside. Instead, Baj heard himself saying, "It's OK. It was an accident."

Once the words had left his lips, Baj felt his shoulders really relax because those words were true and good. He had said the right words for the situation. Baj felt the proud feeling return, and his hand hurt just a little bit less. Mr. Pilma pulled Baj to his feet, and led him toward a bench in the shade. The teacher removed a handkerchief from his pocket and held it firmly to Baj's bleeding palm. Mr. Pilma's brows were furrowed and he was frowning slightly. At first, Baj thought he might be angry with him for hurting himself.

"I'm sorry I got hurt, Mr. Pilma," Baj said sadly. "I guess I didn't see the boys playing. I got into their way." Baj started to cry softly. "Don't be mad at me for ruining things."

At once, Mr. Pilma's face changed. It looked more open, more like he was worried instead of mad. "Baj, I'm not mad at all. I feel concerned about you, and I feel sorry that you got hurt."

"Oh," Baj sniffled. "I'm all confused, I guess." Baj kept taking deep breaths. He felt upset, but in control of himself.

"And another feeling I'm having is pride," Mr. Pilma said.

"Pride?"

"Yes," his teacher nodded with a smile. "I'm proud of you for keeping your cool back there when you got hurt."

Baj looked down at his palm. He checked the handkerchief. The bleeding had stopped. Then he admitted, "I wanted to hit them. I wanted to yell at them. But I couldn't. The Word Launcher wouldn't let me yell at them."

"I bet you were really upset when the boys knocked you down," Mr. Pilma replied.

"I was mad, really mad," Baj said.

"It's interesting to me that you got mad when you got hurt." Mr. Pilma sat back as he spoke. He stretched his feet out in front of him. Baj suspected that Mr. Pilma was getting ready to talk for a while. Baj reflected Mr. Pilma's body as he stretched out his own legs, and leaned back against the bench. *Body reflection* was one of the little tricks that Mr. Pilma had taught Baj to show someone that you were interested in what they were saying. It meant that the listener made his body look sort of like the talker's body. Mr. Pilma was leaning back, so Baj was leaning back a little too.

"I got mad because I thought they knocked me down on purpose," Baj said.

"Hmmm." Mr. Pilma took a moment to think. "Do you still think that they knocked you down on purpose now that you've had some time to think about it?"

"Well, no, I guess not," Baj said.

"What do you think happened?" the teacher asked.

"I think that the boys were playing whiz ball, and I got in the way," Baj admitted. "Not on purpose, of course. By mistake, big mistake."

"I'm curious how big a mistake you think that was," Mr. Pilma said. He looked Baj in the eye. Baj tried to keep looking his teacher in the eye when he answered. Mr. Pilma called it making *eye contact*, which Baj thought was silly because the eyes didn't really make contact. They didn't touch or anything. Or maybe they called it eye contact because of contact lenses that ancient people used to wear before they had corrective vision lasers. Baj couldn't figure that whole thing out, but he tried to make eye contact anyway because it was what people sometimes did when they spoke to each other.

"Like from one to ten? How big a mistake it was from one to ten?" Baj asked. He had rated his feelings with Mr. Pilma before. It was called using a *feelings rating scale*.

"Exactly," Mr. Pilma nodded, and maintained eye contact with Baj. "If 'one' is a little mistake like dropping a piece of paper on a clean floor, and 'ten' is a really big mistake like falling off your bike and breaking your arm, how big is getting knocked down by accident by the boys today?"

Baj looked down at his hand. It still hurt a little. He thought about it for a moment. On one hand, Baj had been hurt kind of bad, but not as bad as a broken arm. On the other hand, it had been an accident.

"I would give it a five or six," Baj finally answered, "because of the blood and all."

"That sounds about right," Mr. Pilma confirmed. "Though when it first happened what rating would you have given it?"

"When it first happened, I thought it was a ten," Baj said emphatically, "even ten plus!"

"What changed your mind?"

"Well," Baj replied thoughtfully, "I guess once I took a moment to stop and think about it, my rating went down. And then it went down a little more when the Word Launcher stopped me from yelling at them."

Mr. Pilma smiled. "You're a good learner, Baj."

"Well, it was the Calming Cape that stopped me from hitting them, not my learning," Baj pushed on.

STOP AND THINK

How does the "feelings rating scale" work?

What does it mean when a mistake is a "one" on the feelings rating scale?

What does a "ten" mean?

Use the feelings rating scale to rate something that is a one on the angry scale.

What about a ten on the angry scale?

Now think of something that is a one on the happy scale.

What would be a ten on the happy scale?

"Actually, Baj," Mr. Pilma said, "the Calming Cape can't really stop your body from moving. You could have hit the boys if you really wanted to. But it did remind you not to make that choice, and then you chose to keep your hands to yourself."

"Really?!"

"Yup." Mr. Pilma stood up. Baj did the same. "How are you feeling now?"

"I feel good about myself for making good choices," Baj said.

"And how is your hand?"

"Actually," Baj said looking down at it, "I had totally forgotten about it."

"Let's swing by the nurse's office, and have her hyper-spray some germ neutralizer and Insta-Heal on it anyway." Mr. Pilma put his arm around Baj's shoulders, and together they walked into the school.

Chapter Nine

Attack of the Laser Scissors

Baj quickly grew comfortable using the full Communication Clarifier Kit, especially as he had hardly taken it off since Mr. Pilma placed the Word Launcher round his neck last week. It didn't take Baj long to sense when the Word Launcher was going to tighten a little around his throat when he was saying something inappropriate. Pretty soon, he was able to guess when the Word Launcher was about to change his words. Baj was learning to adjust what he was going to say even before the Word Launcher had a chance to react.

The Calming Cape continued to be Baj's favorite part of the Communication Clarifier Kit. He had grown to enjoy the warm, gentle pressure on his shoulders and back, and it felt good to Baj to remember that the Calming Cape would always be there for him if he needed help getting control over his feelings.

On most days lately, the Listening Aids hardly whispered any reminders into Baj's ears. Baj couldn't quite figure out how, but he seemed to have learned to understand both the words people said as well as the emotions behind the words. Like sometimes he would be talking to a teacher about some topic that he felt was super interesting, like the inner workings of the gravity releaser mechanism, and he could just tell when the teacher stopped being as interested in the topic as he was. Something might change in the teacher's eyes or direction of her focus. Even if the Listening Aids didn't remind him to avoid talking for too long about one thing, Baj would remember to take a turn at listening instead of speaking.

Mr. Pilma called the long talks that Baj gave *monologues* ("*mono*" means one, as in just one person talking). He encouraged Baj to use more *dialogues* ("*dia*" means two, as in two people talking together) than monologues. The Listening Aids encouraged Baj to do the same thing. Usually, Baj was getting pretty good at remembering all the complicated rules of communication.

Of course, some days were harder than others, and today was a hard day. Baj had woken up feeling grumpy. His head hurt, and he felt like his throat was kind of scratchy. Baj dragged his feet down the hall to the kitchen where his mom was making breakfast.

"Good morning, Baji," his mom said brightly. "I don't have time to toast a bagel the way you like it. Do you mind if I just download a virtual breakfast for you this morning?"

"Actually, I'm not too hungry today," Baj muttered. "Can I just have a meal supplement instead?"

"Sure." Baj's mom plopped down a thin, white wafer on the table in front of Baj. He nibbled on it while he watched her scamper around the kitchen.

Mom's chipper mood suddenly dwindled when she saw Baj's little sister Risa walk into the room. Clearly, Risa had tried out the laser scissors on her hair again. Jagged spikes of blonde hair stood out from her head. Even though Risa's mouth was in a smile, Baj could tell that her eyes looked more worried than pleased.

"Risa! Not again," Baj's mom held her fingers to her mouth. "I told you not to use the laser scissors on your own hair. They are very hard to control."

"Well, I like it," Risa insisted, her lower lip jutting out stubbornly. And to Baj she said, "What are you looking at, monkey butt?"

Baj's eyes narrowed. "Monkey butt? You're the one with the stupid h-h-h..." The rest of his words felt pinched off by the Word Launcher. At the same time, the Calming Cape waved around to embrace his shoulders.

"Yeah, you got something you want to say, monkey butt?" Risa teased him.

"Now, Risa," her mom said as she took her by her arm, "I want you to go to your room right now. And don't come down until you have some control over your mouth. And your hair!"

Risa burst into tears as she rushed from the room.

Just at that moment, Baj's dad came into the kitchen. "Was that a plasma cyclone or a very unhappy girl who just blew by?" his dad joked as he punched in his breakfast order on the food preparator.

"That was our daughter, Plasma Cyclone Risa, after her latest run in with the laser scissors," Mom sighed as she strapped her personal data computer onto her wrist. "But I'm late for work, so I have to run. Please have Risa apologize to her brother for calling him a monkey butt when she comes down. Thanks. Bye, guys." Quick as a wink, Mom was shooting out of the garage toward the rocket station.

"Looks like we have two plasma cyclones in the family this morning," Dad commented as he sat down opposite Baj. When Baj didn't respond, his dad asked, "Hey buddy, you look tired."

"Yeah, I think I am sort of tired," Baj said, "but I feel a little better after my meal supplement."

"You feel well enough to go to school?" Dad asked as he kissed Baj on the forehead. Baj knew his dad was just checking to see if he had a fever, but it still felt good to be kissed by his dad.

"I think so," Baj said. He shifted his gaze over his dad's head. "Don't look now, but here comes Plasma Cyclone Risa."

Risa had wrapped a three-dimensional holographic scarf around her hair, so that it appeared as though cute little kittens were leaping and rolling in a halo around her head.

"Good morning, kittens," Dad said as he patted his daughter on the shoulder. "Would you like to say something to your brother before breakfast?"

"Sorry I called you a monkey butt, Baj," Risa mumbled.

"OK." Baj accepted her apology. Then, with the Word Launcher's help, Baj heard himself say, "Sorry things didn't work out with the laser scissors."

"Thanks." Risa smiled a little as she joined her brother at the table. "Do you think my hair was really as horrible as Mom said?"

Baj anticipated a tightening of the Word Launcher, so he held his tongue while he contemplated an answer. He knew that you had to be very careful about what you said when you were talking about other people's appearance.

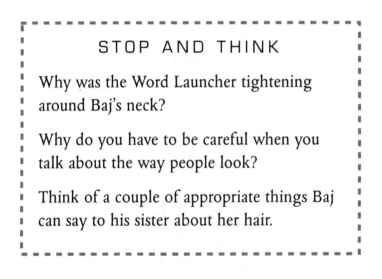

STOP AND THINK

Why was the Word Launcher tightening around Baj's neck?

Why do you have to be careful when you talk about the way people look?

Think of a couple of appropriate things Baj can say to his sister about her hair.

"Well?" Risa asked, searching Baj's face. "Do you?"

"I bet it'll look really cool once it grows in a little," Baj finally said. "Besides, I think your 3D scarf is awesome. Is it new?"

Baj figured he had said the right thing because Risa's face relaxed into a small grin. "Kaje lent it to me yesterday."

"I like it," Baj said.

"Thanks," Risa smiled broadly now.

"OK, troops. Time to boogie." Baj's dad slid open the portal to the garage.

"Boogie?" asked Risa mockingly. "Is that one of your ancient phrases you picked up on Earth when you were in college, Dad?"

"Yeah, *dude*," their dad replied goofily as he danced into the garage. "You know, boogie fever, party hardy, awesome dude."

"Daaaad," Baj and Risa said simultaneously.

"You're silly, Dad," Baj said, even though he was laughing.

In this garage, Baj and his sister strapped themselves onto their flying bikes. Risa hit the go button, and sped off toward school. Baj didn't feel like racing her today. He took his time adjusting his helmet and programming the bike.

"Seriously, Baj," his dad said as he stood next to the transporter pad. He tapped on the transporter control panel and typed in the code to take him to work at his office on the fourth moon. "Give me a call if you don't feel well today, and I'll come pick you up."

"OK, Dad," Baj answered. "I think I'll make it through the day."

"Love you, son," his dad said as he hit the large, blinking *transport now* button on the control panel.

"Love you too, Dad," Baj said to his dad's figure as it became wavy and diluted during transportation. When his father had vanished, Baj pressed the school button on his flying bike, and off he went.

Chapter Ten

Making Mistakes is Part of Learning

(The Hard Part)

Baj tried to focus on Ms. Rrocey's presentation on the history of the Martian Empire in the twenty-fifth century. She had programmed a band of tiny robotic emulators to reenact the Battle of the Ffejry. The rest of the class appeared captivated as the little emulators tumbled and hopped around on the center table, but

Baj's mind wandered. (Plus, he already knew all the details of the Battle of the Ffejry from the electronic history books he pored over whenever he got the chance.)

"Want to be on my team?" Suddenly Anda was asking Baj a question.

"Team? What for?" Baj asked, totally confused.

"For the game, of course," Anda said. When Baj still looked confused, he continued, "Ms. Rrocey wants us to play a history game to help us remember all this Martian stuff."

As Baj looked around the room, he noticed that all the kids seemed to be gathering in small groups around their tables. There were a handful of robotic emulators and two control panels on each table.

Baj didn't know what to do. He hadn't been concentrating when Ms. Rrocey gave the instructions for how to play the game. How was he supposed to know how to play? What if he got all the questions wrong and lost the game for his team? Baj's heart started to beat quickly, and he felt pinpricks of sweat popping out on his forehead. Instantly, the Calming

Cape wrapped an invisible hug around Baj's shoulders, prodding him to take a couple of good deep breaths.

First things first, the Listening Aids whispered in his ear. **Answer your friend's questions.**

Baj looked Anda in the eye. "OK. I'll be on your team."

Anda chuckled, and offered up a hand for Baj to high-five. As the boys' hands smacked, Anda said, "We're going to be a great team, Baj. With all you know about twenty-fifth-century Martian history and my excellent strategy moves, our opponents won't know what hit them."

Anda made a sinister-looking grin, cackled a bit, and rubbed his hands together. Though he looked kind of scary, Baj was pretty sure that Anda wasn't being mean or angry. He was probably just being silly and excited about playing the game.

The Listening Aids confirmed, **Friend is pleased that you are on his team. He hopes to win.**

Anda said, "I'll be right back, Baj. I'm going to find some victims, I mean, *opponents*." Anda's eyes were kind of laughing, so Baj knew that he was just joking about calling them victims. Anda dashed off into the group of students collecting additional supplies for the game.

Baj stood there alone. He felt worried about not knowing how to play the game. He also felt worried about losing. Baj didn't want to disappoint Anda, and he definitely didn't want to lose the game. Playing winning and losing games was something that Mr. Pilma and Baj were still working on. Baj felt slightly relieved by the gentle pressure of the Calming Cape. At least he wouldn't be alone in this hard part of the day. He would have the entire Communication Clarifier Kit on his side.

Baj tapped a finger onto his right Listening Aid as Mr. Pilma had instructed him to do when he wanted to relay information. "I'm worried about this game."

STOP AND THINK

Baj isn't sure how to play the game. What are some of the emotions Baj is feeling right now?

If Baj needs help learning the game, what should he do?

What can you do in class if you don't understand how to do something?

Start at step one, the Listening Aids said. **Find out how to play the game.**

"How am I supposed to do that?" Baj's voiced seemed higher pitched than usual. He was getting a little worked up and panicky.

The teacher is there to help you, the Listening Aids said smoothly.

"But what if she's mad at me for not hearing the directions to the game the first time?" Baj whispered desperately.

The teacher is there to help you, the Listening Aids repeated.

Baj sighed as he started over toward Ms. Rrocey. He stood before her until she finished talking to some other students. When the kids nodded and turned away, Baj knew that it was his turn to talk to the teacher.

"Do you need something, Baj?" Ms. Rrocey asked kindly.

"I…I…" Baj sputtered. Then in a rush, he released his statement. "I'm not sure how to play the game." He didn't tell his teacher that he wasn't listening during her lecture. He wasn't fibbing to her exactly. But still, she didn't need to know why Baj didn't know how to play the game.

"Oh," Ms. Rrocey frowned slightly. "Let me explain it to you again then."

Baj focused as hard as he could on her words as Ms. Rrocey told him how to play the game. He tried to "keep his nervousness out of his ears" (as Mr. Pilma called it when Baj got so nervous about something that he stopped listening). Baj usually found that deep breathing and relaxing using the Calming Cape helped to keep the nervousness out of his ears.

When she came to a part Baj didn't quite understand, the three parts of the Communication Clarifier Kit would work together to remind him to ask more questions until he felt comfortable with her explanation.

"Do you get it now, Baj?" Ms. Rrocey said. She started to walk away, so Baj knew that his time with her was pretty much over.

"I think so," Baj replied.

Ms. Rrocey turned back toward Baj and patted him on the shoulder. She smiled with her eyes and mouth, so he knew she really was pleased. "Once you start playing the game, you'll catch on Baj. I just know." Then she added, "Thanks for asking me to explain it to you better. I think before you got this Communication Clarifier Kit the old Baj would have just gotten really upset and frustrated about the game. Keep up the good work!"

Baj felt pride wash over him. Learning all this new stuff wasn't easy, but at least he was improving a little every day.

When he got back to the table, all the kids were setting up the emulators between them. Anda was busy programming their battle strategy into the computer. He turned to Baj and asked, "What's the name of that big crater on Mars, the one on the lower equator?"

Baj was thrilled that he knew the answer (the Veronica Horizon Crater, of course!), and soon he too became caught up in the game.

Thirty minutes later, the game was neck and neck, a tie. Baj and Anda made some excellent moves with their emulators, but their opponents, their friends Cundan and Nniae, were very strong players too. It was going to be a close game, and Baj wasn't sure that he and Anda would win.

The Calming Cape was wrapped tightly around Baj's shoulders. The Listening Aids were whispering more than usual reminders into his ears. Still, he was feeling really upset and scared about the possibility of losing the game.

Anda, Cundan, and Nniae were talking and laughing all at once. They were all working really hard on winning the game, but they seemed to think it was fun at the same time, even though somebody was going to lose. Baj couldn't really understand how they could just seem so happy and relaxed while they were playing a win–lose game. He wished that he could feel that way too. He knit his brows in determination to get better at not worrying so much about losing a game.

Cundan and Nniae huddled over their control panel, contemplating their next move. Anda said to them, "You'd better watch out 'cause we're going to turn you into Martian dust!" Anda's voice was tough, but his eyes were bright. Cundan and Nniae smiled.

Nniae said, "You wish, little grolfling! Don't bet on it." She giggled as she punched in the final code on the control panel, sending the emulators into a flurry of activity.

Baj's friends' words were tough, and they were acting serious about playing the game. But then they would laugh and joke as the emulators tumbled over the game board, taking or losing new ground. Baj felt very confused. Anda, Cundan, and Nniae seemed to be having a great time playing. Meanwhile, Baj was becoming more and more distressed as it looked like he and Anda might lose the game.

Baj turned to his friend. Anda was totally captivated by the movement of the emulators.

Blast! One of their players got vaporized by the opposing team. Anda grunted with disappointment, but he didn't seem to be overly sad about it. "It doesn't look good for us, buddy," Anda said to Baj as they decided what move to make next.

"I'm sorry," Baj's head sank onto his chest. He could feel tears prickling his eyes. "Are you really mad?"

"Of course not, Baj." Anda poked Baj with his elbow. "It's just a dumb ol' game."

"I don't think this game is fun at all," Baj replied sadly. He wanted to say that he hated the game. He wanted to wipe all the emulators right off the board, but the Communication Clarifier Kit helped him keep control over his body and his words.

"Really?" Anda seemed genuinely surprised. "I love it. I hope Ms. Rrocey lets us play again tomorrow during history time."

Now Baj was really confused. "You *love* it?" he asked Anda. "But we're going to lose the game! How can you love it?"

"I don't know," Anda answered. "I just do. It's fun. Besides, I've been paying attention to

Cundan and Nniae's strategy. I think we can beat them next time."

Baj wanted to say that he thought the game was the worst game in the world. But the Word Launcher tightened around his neck slightly. Baj realized that would be an exaggeration and was a little surprised to hear himself saying, "Maybe I'll try playing this game one more time."

"Cool," Anda answered. "It beats reading all those chapters in the school ebooks, and answering those boring comprehension questions they ask."

Baj thought he preferred reading the ebooks, and he actually liked figuring out the answers to the questions, but he didn't say so.

As Baj had feared, his team lost the Martian battle game. Cundan and Nniae whooped and hollered as they celebrated their victory. Anda pounded the table in defeat. He looked disappointed for a moment, but then he started to smile. "I challenge you to a re-match!" Anda declared pointing across the table.

Nniae smiled, "Accepted. Same time, same place. Tomorrow."

Then Baj joined in the fun of a friendly competition. He chuckled a little. Even if he couldn't feel the same relaxed attitude about losing, at least he could *try* to join in their fun. So Baj said, "We'll be there. Just watch out. We're going to blast you to Martian dust!"

The way his friends all laughed, Baj could tell that they knew he was just kidding around. Anda whispered in Baj's ear, "Next time, it's our turn to win!"

"For sure," Baj heard himself agree, and then he thought, "Even if we lose again, we'll still have a good time."

STOP AND THINK

How did Cundan and Nniae feel about winning?

What were some of the emotions that Anda had about losing?

Why did the Communication Clarifier Kit help Baj keep himself from knocking all the emulators off the game board?

What did Baj learn about winning and losing games?

Chapter Eleven

Taking Off the Cape

"Well? Are you going to let me see the cape on you?" asked Anda. "You promised that you would show me the cape."

Baj looked at the holographic image of Anda's face as it was projected by the holo-gramphone in Baj's bedroom. Anda seemed genuinely excited about the Communication Clarifier Kit. Still, Baj had been really apprehensive about sharing the kit with his best friend. He had learned so much from the Listening Aids, the Calming Cape, and the Word Launcher since Mr. Pilma had given them to him a month ago.

Baj had learned about using people's body language as well as their words to understand what they were trying to say. He had learned about keeping his cool by deep breathing and relaxation, so he could really hear what people were saying. He was working on not getting so lost in his nervousness or anger, so he could use his words to solve problems. The Word Launcher had really helped Baj to stop and think before he spoke, and when he did speak he would try to say appropriate and reasonable words for the situation. This stuff was not easy, but Baj was improving more and more every day.

Baj felt very proud of himself, and especially proud that Mr. Pilma thought that he wouldn't need to use the Communication Clarifier Kit any longer. Already, the Listening Aids were scarcely ever whispering in Baj's ears because he was getting better at understanding people's words and their meaning. He could hardly remember the last time he needed the Calming Cape, except during that bad day at school last week. (Baj had woken up with a fever the next morning. Mr. Pilma said that getting sick could make communicating tons harder.) Baj still used the Word Launcher now and then, mostly for times when he was really angry or scared or confused. But he could imagine the day coming soon when he wouldn't really need it anymore.

Baj had decided to share the Communication Clarifier Kit with Anda before he had to start giving it back to Mr. Pilma. He wanted to share this important part of his life with his best friend. Plus he thought that Anda would think it was totally amazing that Baj got to wear all the cool stuff all the time. So Baj slowly put on the Calming Cape.

"Wow!" Anda sighed. "You are so lucky to get to wear that cape. You're like a secret super sleuth."

Baj smiled broadly. He and Anda were really into stories about spies and detectives, but being a secret super sleuth, that was the best of all.

"Too bad I have to start giving this stuff back to Mr. Pilma," Baj said into the hologramphone.

"Why do you have to give it back?" Anda asked.

"Well," Baj began, "I guess I don't really need it too much anymore."

"That's a good thing, right?" his best friend asked.

"Yeah," Baj laughed. "That's a good thing."

"Hey!" Anda jumped up suddenly. "My mom bought some of that holographic material, like your sister's kitten headband! Why don't you come over, and we can make our own super sleuth capes!"

"Great idea." Baj jumped up too, grabbing his backpack. "Should I bring the Communication Clarifier Kit?"

"Nah," Anda said. "I don't think you're going to need it. We're going to do just fine."

Baj smiled to himself as he clicked off the hologramphone. Anda was right, Baj was going to do just fine.